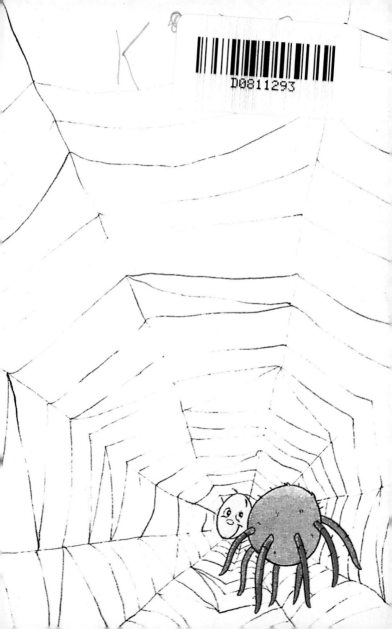

ISBN 1 85534 567 6

Printed and bound in Slovenia.

The Boy Who Cried "Wolf!"

Retold by Judy Hamilton

Illustrated by Lindsay Duff

Tarantula Books

In a small village which nestled among the mountains there once lived a young shepherd boy. It was his job to tend to the village flock, taking the sheep to their grazing ground every day and returning them to their fold at night. In summer time, the shepherd boy had to take the sheep high up above the village to the mountain pastures to graze, but every night he still had to bring them back to the village for safety; there were wolves on the mountain side, who could attack the sheep on the pastures at night.

The shepherd boy enjoyed his work most of the time, but there were times when he would get a little lonely, high on the mountainside all day with no-one to keep him company.

One day towards the end of summer, the shepherd boy was sitting amongst his sheep in the sweet mountain grass, looking down at the village below him. He could see the tiny figures of the children playing in the village square. He could see the women bustling about preparing for market day. And in the fields outside the village, he could see the men hard at work tending to the crops which were nearly ready to harvest. Everybody had someone to talk to and to work beside. Of all the villagers, the shepherd boy was the only one who had to work alone. It did not seem fair.

He looked round at the sheep, peacefully munching the grass. He was fond of them, but they could not talk to him or make him laugh.

The shepherd boy was terribly bored. Nothing exciting ever happened. There were supposed to be wolves on the mountain, but he had never seen one. Nobody had seen any wolves for a very long time . . .

Suddenly the shepherd boy had an idea. He knew how to liven things up a bit. He jumped to his feet and ran down the mountainside a little way towards the village. Taking a deep breath, he cupped his hands round his mouth and yelled with all his might:

"WOLF!-WOLF!"

Down below in the village, the people heard the distant calls of the shepherd boy and were filled with alarm. Everybody stopped what he or she was doing. The workers in the fields gathered together their hoes and rakes to use as weapons. The women grabbed their sweeping brushes. The children found sticks to wave in the air. Then the whole village hurried up the mountainside to the aid of the shepherd boy.

It was a hot day and the mountain was very steep, but the villagers climbed as fast as they could. When they reached the high pastures, they looked around for the wolf, but could see none. The sheep were grazing peacefully, and the shepherd boy was laughing heartily.

When the villagers realized that the shepherd boy had played a trick on them, they were very angry indeed.

"That was a very stupid thing to do!" they told him. "We have wasted precious working time!"

The shepherd boy told them he was very sorry, although secretly he thought that his trick had been a great success. He had enjoyed it very much!

"Don't try anything like that again," an old man warned him. "One day you might really need our help, and find that no-one is willing to help you."

The villagers left the shepherd boy and went back down the mountainside, still angry.

Time passed. For many days the shepherd boy found that he was still unpopular with the villagers, but after a while they forgave him and life returned to normal. Every day as usual the shepherd boy led the sheep up the mountain and watched over them till evening, when he drove them back down to their pen in the village. He still felt that life was rather too quiet for his liking, alone on the mountain, but whenever he felt bored he remembered the trick he had played on the villagers and had a good laugh to himself.

However, the days dragged slowly by, and the shepherd boy became more and more restless.

His boredom became almost unbearable. He was tired of playing the same old tunes on the whistle that he carried with him, but he could not be bothered to make up any new ones. He tried singing to the sheep but they didn't pay any attention. He tried to while away the hours making daisy chains, but after a time his fingers began to hurt, and the daisies only wilted.

He remembered how funny it had been to watch all the villagers charging up the mountain brandishing their weapons when he had called for help. It would be such fun to see it all again, just one more time.

Just as he had done before, the shepherd boy went a little way down the mountainside and began to shout at the top of his voice:

"WOLF!" he called. "WOLF! HELP! WOLF!"

Down below in the village, the people heard the shouts of the shepherd boy, but this time they hesitated before they went to help him.

The workers in the fields looked at one another.

"That's the shepherd boy calling," said one. "Do you think it's another joke?"

"I'm not sure," said another. "He may really be in trouble this time."

Reluctantly, the villagers decided that they could not ignore the shepherd boy.

Once more, they gathered what weapons they could and started the hard trek up the mountainside. When they arrived at the pasture ground, they were very hot and out of breath. Just as before, the sheep appeared unconcerned and cropped the grass contentedly. There was no sign of a wolf anywhere.

"Where is the wolf?" demanded one of the men. The helpless laughter of the shepherd boy told him all that he needed to know. The young scoundrel had played the same trick on them as before.

The villagers had been angry enough the last time that this had happened, but this time they were absolutely furious.

"You are a stupid and selfish boy!" they shouted. "It is harvest time, and we have more than our fair share of work to do in the fields, yet you call us all the way up here on a false alarm!"

Once again, the shepherd boy apologised for the trouble he had caused, and this time he really meant it. He could see how angry the villagers were, and he also noticed how tired some of the older people looked after their long climb up the mountain.

"I am truly sorry to have caused you all so much trouble," he said to them humbly.

But the villagers only looked at him suspiciously. They did not believe him.

It was a long time before anybody in the village would speak to the shepherd boy. Finally, they grudgingly made friends with him again. But the old man who had warned him about his tricks shook his head sadly.

"It may be too late now," was all that he said.

Life followed its usual pattern for some weeks. Then one day, while the shepherd boy was lying in the pasture daydreaming, he saw the most frightening sight. Not one, but TWO huge wolves were running towards the sheep, snarling and gnashing their teeth.

The shepherd boy was terrified. He knew that he was no match for these ferocious beasts. Getting to his feet, he ran down the hill as fast as his legs would carry him.

Once within earshot of the village, he called out as loud as he could.

"HELP! HELP! WOLVES!" his cries reached the workers in the fields. But nobody moved.

"COME QUICK! THEY ARE KILLING THE SHEEP!" he called, loud enough for the rest of the village to hear. But nobody paid any attention. The shepherd boy kept calling and calling, but nobody came. Nobody believed him. He turned back up the hill. When he reached the pasture, the sheep were all dead and the wolves had gone. Sadly, the shepherd boy returned to the village alone. The villagers would never trust him to look after their sheep again. He had cried "WOLF!" once too often.